T0197532

One Shoe On
and One Shoe Off

JIM JOHNSON

Illustrated by
Izabela Ciesinska
Bloomington, Indiana

Angela, Tonya, James Jr., Kenosha, Grover IV, Masai, Devon,

Mikisa, U'Maru, Kristy, Roshawn, Prentis Jr., Janae, Jason, Jade,

Sage, Koloneus, Savion, Kia, Alexis, James III-Tra, Sah-ji, Leroy Jr.,

Anna, Christina, Marcus, Jasmin, Justice, Tayja, Masaunique, Sania,

Masai Jr., Q'Mari, Lakisha, Shanell, Jhordon, A'Mir, Le'Auja, TaTa.

A special thank you to my family.

I love you all!

To order additional copies of this book, contact:
Xlibris
844-714-8691
www.Xlibris.com
Orders@Xlibris.com

ISBN: Softcover   978-1-4415-5560-1
            EBook   978-1-4771-7515-6

Print information available on the last page

Rev. date: 01/09/2023

Thank you

Shannon and Rachel O'Leary, Brennor and Sue Beck, Dan and Karen Williams, Dave Olson and Family, John Coley, Are and Dale, Brad and Margaret Holmstrom, Bea Bastian, Skip Young and family, Nancy Gonzales and Marisa (Dollie), Kris and Mari, John Sommer and Sam Stevens' families, Mike and Elizabeth Lodjic, Steve and Kaitlyn Williams, Tom, Phil and Maryann Spence, Art Budd, Gregg and Teresa Schmitz, Nate and Gerlinda Hackney, Shot and Linda Pryor, Dave and Nancy Crittenden, Cheryl Hanna-Triscott (Photo), The Subia family, Heidi and Janet—Early Head Start—Gig Harbor Wa. Patty at Braeside Cabin in beautiful Estes Park Colorado, Izzi (Another beautiful job), Ann Sundgren (Teach), and Ben, Barb York, Doug and Sue Cole, Steve and Mary Adams, Lynne Adam, Kevin, Brett, Bee Jay, Clarence, Dan, Greg, Mark, Chuck, John Bare, Kiwanis Club of Peninsula – Gig Harbor Wa., The Evergreen State College – Tacoma Wa.

One shoe on and one shoe off,

I think my other one is lost!

Help me find my other shoe,

so I can go and play with you!

Mother says, it's nice today,

you can go outside and play!

Please help Bobby find his shoe,

so he can go and play with you!

Bobby looks to find his shoe. He thinks
to himself, "I haven't a clue."
He looks over here and looks over there,
"Maybe the closet," he says to himself!

Bobby looks all around, here and
there, and up and down!
"I want to go and play with you,
but I can't find my other shoe!"

Running shoes, tennis shoes, big
shoes and small, brown shoes,
black shoes, yellow shoes all!
Mommy shoes, Daddy shoes,
and Brother shoes too. Sister
shoes here, red, green, and blue!

Brother wears shoes for sport
and play, Sister wears hers for
dance and ballet!
Mother wears hers for shopping
for clothes, Daddy wears boots
while working on roads!

Bobby screams, "I found my shoe.

Now I can go and play with you!"

Bobby's glad he found his shoe,

now he will go and play with you!

First put your socks on, left foot right. Then put your shoes on, tie them tight!

We use our shoes for work

and play, run and walk

and jump each day!

Don't forget to wear your shoes,

but always remember

the "Golden Rule"!

One shoe on and one shoe off,

I thought my other one was lost.

You helped me find my other

shoe.

Now I will go and play with you!

Printed in the United States
by Baker & Taylor Publisher Services